JUST

You are cordially invited

to

GRANDMA BEETLE'S
BIRTHDAY PARTY!

Please Sunday

IN CASE

A Trickster Tale
and Spanish Alphabet Book

Yuyi Morales

A NEAL PORTER BOOK
ROARING BROOK PRESS
NEW YORK

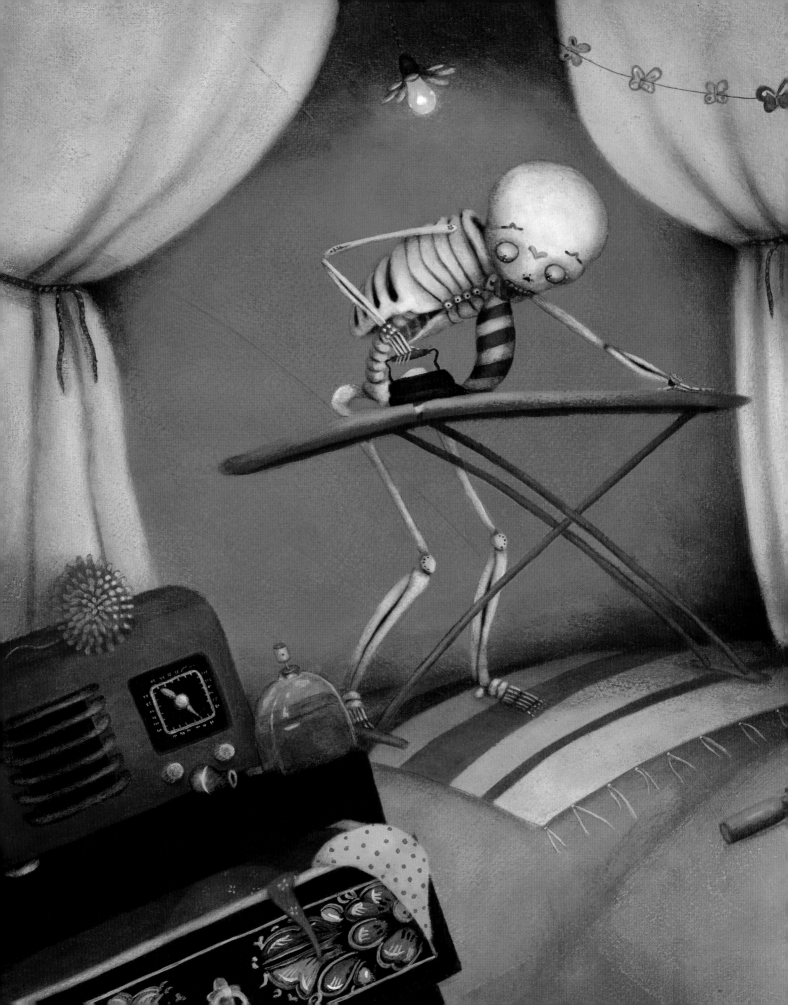

At last the day had arrived. It was Grandma Beetle's birthday!

Señor Calavera put on cologne, dusted his hat, ironed his best tie, and pumped the tires of his bike.

Grandma Beetle was Señor Calavera's friend. And her last party had been a blast. He would not miss this one for anything in the world.

7

Noviembre

CIEN AÑOS DE SOLEDAD

Riding through the neighborhood with glee, he waved good-bye to his friends. Soon he would be at Grandma's. Oh, *si*!

Then, a moan from beyond the grave—

"Juuuuuust a miiiinute!"

—nearly made him fall.
What a fright!

But it was only Zelmiro the Ghost.
"Going to Grandma Beetle's party?"
Señor Calavera tipped his hat.
"She will be glad that you are right
on time. But aren't you forgetting
something?"

Señor Calavera scratched his head.
He had done everything he was
supposed to do.

Unless . . .
¿Quizás?
Oh, my. He had forgotten a
present for Grandma Beetle!

"Don't worry." Zelmiro
smiled. "You surely must
know, the best present to
give a friend is the thing
she would love the most."

Of course!
Señor Calavera went
looking and chose
especially for
Grandma Beetle . . .

Un **A**cordeón.
An accordion for her to dance to.

Bigotes.
A mustache
because she had none.

Cosquillas.
Tickles to make her laugh.

COSQUILLAS
Para Toda Ocasión

Un **CH**iflido.
A whistle he trapped in a bag.

The ghost clapped. "Your gifts are a vision!"
Señor Calavera hummed while he tied the
presents to his bike.

"But, I wonder," Zelmiro said, "are they what
Grandma Beetle would love the most? Why don't
you look again, my friend? Just in case . . ."

Señor Calavera thought for a moment. He still
had some time.

So, he searched once more and packed . . .

Dientes.
Teeth for a good bite.

Una **E**scalera.
A ladder to reach past the sky.

Una **F**lauta.
A flute he made from a branch.

Granizado.
A snow cone flavored with syrup.

"Your presents stop me cold!" The ghost squirmed in delight.

Señor Calavera didn't know he could be so good at finding presents!

"But, I wonder," Zelmiro said, "are they what Grandma Beetle would love the most? Why don't you look again, my friend? Just in case . . ."

It wasn't late yet, Señor Calavera realized.

So, he poked around and picked . . .

Una **H**istorieta.
A one-of-a-kind comic book.

Instrucciones.
Instructions to find all things lost.

Para encontrar algo
perdido siga estas
instrucciones al pie de
la letra:

1) haga bizcos con los ojos.

Un **J**aguar.
A jaguar to keep her safe.

Un **K**ilo.
More than two pounds
for balance and
weight.

I kilo

"Your gifts move my soul." The ghost gave a bow.
Señor Calavera was ready without a doubt!
"But, I wonder," Zelmiro said, "are they what
Grandma Beetle would love the most? Why don't you
look again, my friend? Just in case . . ."
Señor Calavera frowned; being on time was his job.
Still, he hustled and found . . .

Una **L**otería.
A lottery game to play
with her grandchildren.

LA MASCARA

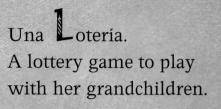

LOTERIA

Una **Ll**ave.
A key to open all doors.

EL METATE

EL ANGEL

Un **M**oño.
A bow to tie her hair.

Niebla.
Fog, to play
hide-and-seek in.

The ghost gasped. "Your presents make my heart stop."
Grandma is going to be surprised!

"But, I wonder," Zelmiro said, "are they what Grandma
Beetle would love the most? Why don't you look again, my
friend? Just in case . . ."

Grandma must already be icing the cake! Even so, she
deserved the best.

So Señor Calavera sought and chose . . .

Ñapa.
A little extra of everything.

Un Ombligo.
A bread called
belly button.

Un **P**apalote.
A kite to play with
the wind.

Quince años.
Fifteen more
years of life.

The ghost gave a cheer.
"Your gifts are to die for!"
Señor Calavera hopped onto
his bike.
Zelmiro took a deep breath.
"But, I wonder," he said. "Are
they what Grandma Beetle
would love the most? Why
don't you look again, my
friend? Just in case . . ."
Surely Grandma's beautiful
grandchildren must already be
at the party! Señor Calavera
quickly went looking
and got . . .

Rayuela.
Her favorite childhood game.

Una **S**emilla.
A seed to plant and grow.

Un **T**itere.
A puppet made
from a sock.

Uñas.
Fingernails
fierce and strong.

"Your gifts take my breath away." The ghost sighed.
Señor Calavera looked at his watch. He didn't want to
miss breaking the piñatas!
Zelmiro studied the presents on the bike. "But, my friend,
I wonder," he said, "are they what Grandma Beetle would
love the most? Look again. Just in case . . ."
Even though it was already late, Señor Calavera ran to
pick out . . .

Vainilla.
A fragant vanilla pod.

Una **W**,
to have two *v*'s for
when one is not enough.

Una **X**ilografía.
Wood engraved art
to hang in her room.

El Santo Vive

Yerbabuena.
A good herb to soothe her day.

And . . .

Nothing more!

Señor Calavera had taken too long.
He was going to miss the party!
He climbed onto his bike and
hurried off before Zelmiro could ask
anything else.

COSQUILLAS
Para Toda Ocasión

Look at Señor Calavera pedaling so fast!

Oh, no. Watch out, Señor Calavera!
Oh, dear!
Poor Señor Calavera.
All of his beautiful presents—ruined.

Señor Calavera couldn't believe
his misfortune.
    And now there was no time left
to get any presents at all. Except . . .

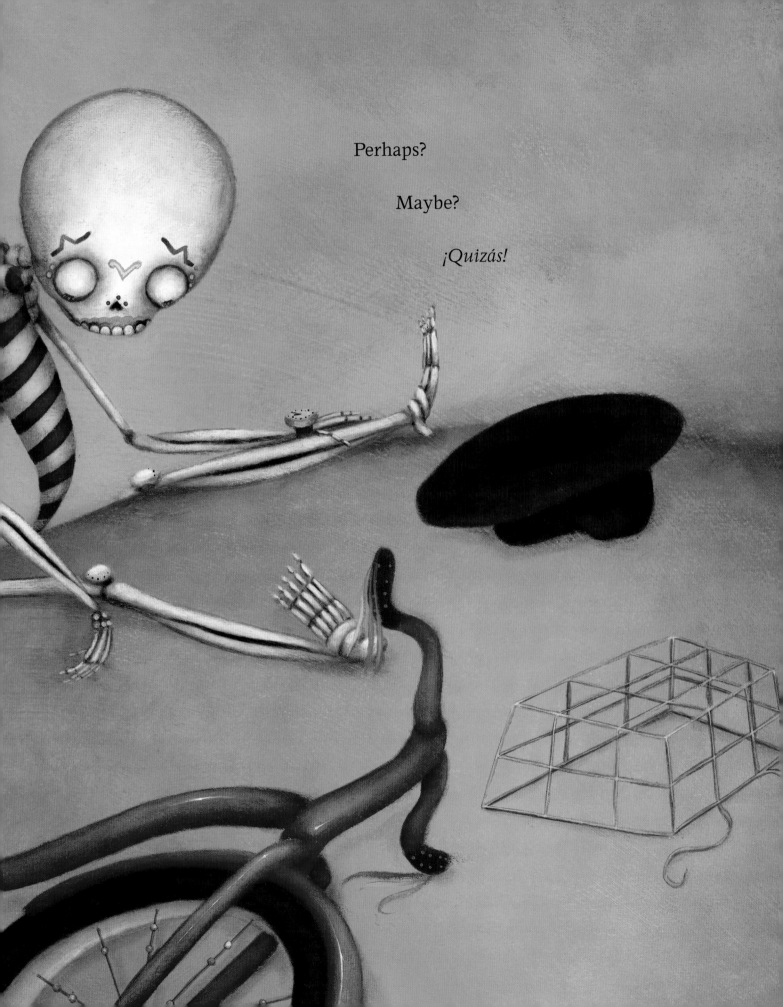

Perhaps?

Maybe?

¡Quizás!

When Grandma Beetle was about to
blow out the candles on her cake, she
heard a knock at the door and, oh my!
Waiting for her she found . . .

. . . Señor Calavera, who had brought Grandma Beetle the present she loved the most.

"Grandpa

To Tim, who gave me the idea for this story
while we held hands in the old and sizzling city of Veracruz.

A Neal Porter Book

Published by Roaring Brook Press

Roaring Brook Press is a division of Holtzbrinck Publishing Holdings Limited Partnership

175 Fifth Avenue, New York, New York 10010

mackids.com

Library of Congress Cataloging-in-Publication Data

Morales, Yuyi.

Just in case / Yuyi Morales. — 1st ed.

p. cm.

Summary: As Senor Calavera prepares for Grandma Beetle's birthday he finds an alphabetical assortment

of unusual presents, but with the help of Zelmiro the Ghost, he finds the best gift of all.

ISBN 978-1-59643-329-8

[1. Birthdays—Fiction. 2. Gifts—Fiction. 3. Ghosts—Fiction. 4. Alphabet—Fiction.] I. Title.

PZ7.M7881927Ju 2008

[E]—dc22

2007044061

Roaring Brook Press books are available for special promotions and premiums.

For details, contact: Director of Special Markets, Holtzbrinck Publishers.

Printed in China by RR Donnelley Asia Printing Solutions Ltd., Dongguan City, Guangdong Province

First edition August 2008

6   8   10   9   7

37 — LA MASCARA

20 — LOS DIABLITOS

13 — EL LIBRO

21 — EL CHOCOLATE

22 — EL BALERO

4 — EL CHUPIRUL

2 — EL MAROMERO

26 — EL MORRALITO

54 — EL ANGEL